Nina Ring Aamundsen

Two Short and One Long

Houghton Mifflin Company
Boston 1990

J
AAmundse

Copyright © 1990 by Nina Ring Aamundsen

All rights reserved. For information about permission
to reproduce selections from this book, write to
Permissions, Houghton Mifflin Company, 2 Park Street,
Boston, Massachusetts 02108.

Printed in the United States of America

BP 10 9 8 7 6 5 4 3 2 1

Library of Congress Cataloging-in-Publication Data

Aamundsen, Nina Ring, 1945–
    [To korte og en lang. English]
    Two short and one long / Nina Ring Aamundsen ; translated by the
author. — 1st American ed.
        p. cm.
    Translation of: To korte og en lang.
    Summary: Best friends Jonas and Einar, two Norwegian boys, must
come to terms with each other and their prejudices when a large
Afghanistan family moves into the neighborhood.
    ISBN 0-395-52434-2
    [1. Friendship—Fiction. 2. Prejudices—Fiction. 3. Norway—
Fiction.] I. Title.
PZ7.A1118Tw   1990   90-4545
[Fic]—dc20   CIP
                          AC

This one is for Annie and Martin

Acknowledgments

I am grateful for all the help I received from class 6A 1985–86 at Kihle school, Kapp, Østre Toten and their teacher, Bjørg Broberg. And to Josef Skullerud, Kapp, for his assistance, too. I also want to thank class 4B 1986–87 at Lilleborg school in Oslo and their teacher, Grethe Moe. And finally, I am grateful beyond measure to Charlotte Vale Allen for her enthusiastic support and invaluable help with bringing this book into English. Thank you.

O N E

ONLY ONE MORE week and the summer holidays would be over. Einar and I were standing near the subway kiosk, eating potato chips out of a giant bag. The bag crackled, and when we shook out the last crumbs it felt as if I'd swallowed half the Gobi Desert. A quick but thorough search of all our pockets — including Einar's shoe, where he always keeps a krone — turned up just enough for us to split a Coke. Good.

We were sitting on the railing, dangling our legs toward Veitvetveien. It was hot, hot. Summer had come at the beginning of July this year, the day before my family went to the

1

countryside. The sun shone day after day, and summer went on and on. I could easily have started another holiday and gone back to school in October. Just thinking about it made me sigh. Einar, who always seems to read my mind, sighed too. In a week, everything would be over.

With two short and one long burp we finished the Coke, and Einar put the deposit money from returning the Coke bottle back in his shoe. "Safe as a bank," he said, and meant it. Einar is my best friend.

I have lived at Veitvet all my life: Jonas Oliver Bakken, age twelve, Erich Mogensønsvei 4B, three floors up and the door to the right, Oslo, Norway, Scandinavia, Europe, Western Hemisphere, the world, inner space — that's me.

We stayed in the shade under the subway crossover and watched the traffic up and down Veitvetveien. It wasn't very exciting. The doors behind us opened from time to time when the Undergrounders came out. My sister calls them that. She's a little kid, only five, and thinks everybody gets on the trains in the morning, works underground all day, then turns around and comes home again. That's Kara.

A blue Volkswagen Variant station wagon

2

drove past. Two beds and two mattresses were tied onto the roof. The car was full of chairs, and the driver was trapped by the chair legs.

"Someone's moving," Einar said.

"Mmmn," said I.

The car turned onto Beverveien and went out of sight. A Mazda with a dining table and three mattresses came by, following the other mattresses.

"Someone's moving," I said.

"Mmmn," said Einar.

We pulled our arms free from the railing and went out into the warm sunshine. I tried to look straight at the sun but had to close my eyes after a couple of seconds. Even with my eyes closed, everything was sun and whiteness. When I opened them again, the world was full of silvery shadows, and I had to grab hold of Einar's arm until everything went back to its usual color and shape.

Einar Andersen's hair was bleached white by the sun. If you're ever wondering what kind of summer we've had, just take a look at Einar's hair. If it's white, the summer was a good one. If it's yellow, we had only rain. I love holidays anyway, and now there was only one week left.

We crossed Veitvetveien and went down Beverveien, past the garages. Tracking the mattresses. We found them outside number nine, spread on the grass outside the corner flat. We approached silently and carefully.

Einar is a year older than I am, but we're in the same grade at school. He's also much shorter than I am. Sometimes people call us Salt and Pepper because Einar's hair is as light as mine is dark. Einar gets awfully mad when they call us that, so we usually chase the pests up the nearest tree. Since trees are scarce at Veitvet, we all get our constitutionals.

My paternal grandmother always says that my great-great-great-grandfather was a pirate. When I was a little kid I thought a lot about that, and I still do from time to time. My whole family has light blond hair, except me. So I guess I'm the only one who takes after my distant grandfather. I used to daydream a lot about my pirate family, that some summer day they'd come and cast anchor in the bay. They'd send a small rowboat ashore to get me and take me off with them on their next expedition — to Spain or maybe to South America. My whole pirate family would be on board, and every one of them would have the same dark hair as mine, and their skin would be very brown, tanned by the rough life on the sea. They wouldn't be pirates anymore, though. More like Gypsies,

4

Gypsies of the seven seas. They'd have a very old ship — a beautiful three-master.

Granny and Grandpa are from Kapp, on the Mjøsa, the biggest lake in Norway, as it says in my geography book. My father's from Kapp too, of course, and so is my uncle Peder, who took over running the farm from Granny and Grandpa. Dad is an engine driver, on the Røros line. There's nothing much of the pirate about him. But who ever heard of pirates on Mjøsa?

"Foreigners," said Einar. "Pakistani."

"Yes," I answered. "Or maybe pirates." I whispered the words so low he didn't hear.

Lots of kids were carrying things into the house. Two men were unloading the cars. A couple of women came out on the stairs every few minutes and said something in a language I didn't understand. Pirate language?

It was incredible, all the things they'd managed to get into the two cars. And when they were finally emptied, everyone sat down on the grass and had a glass of lemonade and some cookies. Or maybe they were crackers. Suddenly, I was very thirsty, and I took a few steps toward them. They looked at us. They nodded. I nodded.

"Hi."

"Hi."

Difficult to find anything more to say. My brain was gone. Nobody home. I felt stupid, but I still didn't move because I wanted to talk to them. Einar grabbed me by the arm, indicating that he wanted to go. Okay, we went.

The two cars passed us a while later when we were sitting on the stairs to the shopping center. An arm waved to us from the Variant. I waved back. Einar just looked sulky. It was almost dinnertime.

"I forgot my jacket at your place." Einar looked at me with his light blue eyes.

That made me laugh. He was always forgetting something at my place. "Come on, then," I said, giving him a friendly slap on the back. "Last one home's a sissy."

And we ran through the sunshine. Up the steep hill. Then across to my building. As usual, Einar got there first, and we sat down in the cool entrance to my building to get our breath back.

"Do you think they'll all be moving into number nine?" I asked after a while.

"Maybe. I don't know," said Einar. "What time is it?"

"Nearly four."

"Gotta run. See you." And then he was gone.

On my way upstairs I remembered that he still hadn't taken his jacket. But I knew he'd be back as soon as he'd had dinner. Einar always comes back.

T W O

D INNER WAS COOKING on the stove, and everybody was shouting at each other in the living room when I got in.

"I can't stand it any longer. That monkey is driving me nuts. Get it out of here! OUT!" That was Dad. He was angry.

Kara was standing by the stereo. She was angry too. "I want to hear the song about Julius the monkey, but I don't want to hear the other songs. I hate them. They're silly. You have to rewind the cassette for me because I don't want to hear anything *but* Julius. It's my cassette. I can do what I want!"

"But you've got to understand that I can't listen to that ape twenty times in a row. I want my dinner. I want some peace and quiet. I want to rest. I'm tired."

Mum cut in and said she was sure Kara could borrow my cassette player and listen to her tape in the bedroom, so we could all have some peace. Mum looked at me pleadingly. I nodded and went to get the cassette player, my birthday present. Kara sat in the middle of Mum and Dad's bed, and I showed her how to use the machine.

"You have to help me rewind the tape," she said, wiping away her angry tears.

I said, "Sure," and shut the door behind me as I left the room. I can't stand that monkey song either.

Finally dinner was ready. Vegetable soup. That's okay. In fact, I like it. Kara likes only about half the vegetables, and she always has a hard time separating the carrots, the potatoes, the cauliflower, the leek, the celery root, and the peas. It takes her ages to eat a small bowl of vegetable soup because the bits keep drifting together and messing up her system. I closed my eyes and ears and ate really fast. Kara wouldn't be finished with her dinner until long after I'd left the table.

While we ate I told everyone about the new

family in Beverveien. They didn't seem to be listening until I said they were Pakistani.

"How nice," said Mum. "Did you speak to them?"

"Just said hello."

"How do you know they're Pakistani?" she asked. "There are a lot of countries in Asia, and Pakistan's only one of them."

"No, I don't really know," I said, and felt kind of dumb. "I just thought they were."

"Any children?" Mum wasn't giving up yet. "Any kids your age?"

"Lots," I laughed, remembering them all sitting out on the grass.

"All immigrants have lots of children," Dad said. "Too many."

This was the first thing he'd said in a long time. In fact, he hadn't said a word since he'd chased Julius out of the living room.

"Harald," Mum said, "you shouldn't joke about things like that."

Dad didn't look as if he was joking. He looked cross.

"Well, they do, don't they? Have a lot of children, I mean. You can't understand what they're saying, and they smell bad too."

"What is the matter with you today, Harald?"

My dad sighed heavily. "Overtime this weekend."

"Then why don't you say so and stop talking rubbish!"

It was clear that Mum was worked up and wasn't going to calm down for a while, so I ate even faster.

"What," Mum started, "has a newly moved-in Pakistani family got to do with your working overtime? Can you explain that to me?"

He couldn't. He didn't even try.

"And," she went on, "how many sisters do I have, my dear Harald? How many?"

"Four," Dad answered, sounding defeated.

To tell the truth, Mum is proud of her family. There are five children, all girls, and Mum is number three. Two pairs of twins, so Mum's an only child. That's what she likes to say. Before Kara was born, she kept insisting it would be twins because they run in the family. Boy, am I glad we don't have Kara in stereo.

I'd had as much as I could take, so I left the kitchen. I don't think anybody even noticed. All of them were so absorbed in the family quarrel. I like to stay out of family arguments, but usually, and secretly, I side with Dad. Even when he's wrong. Or maybe because he's wrong.

We have only two bedrooms in our apartment, but I still have a room of my own, to the right just inside the front door. Kara sleeps in the closet. Well, it used to be a closet. You have to go through it to get to Mum and Dad's room. But it's pretty big and Kara's happy with it, except when she starts saying she wants my room. She'll never get it.

Our living room is like any other, but we're going to be getting a balcony. This year every apartment in Veitvet is getting a balcony. Ours is being built right outside the living room and the big bedroom. Mum's very pleased about it because she's always worrying Kara will fall out the window. With a balcony it wouldn't be that far to fall. "That kid's going to drive me crazy one day," she complains whenever Kara pretends she's a squirrel or some other kind of light-footed animal.

I was glad when Einar rang the doorbell. There's nothing like killing time with Einar. And we had decided to waste all the time we had until Monday.

When I opened the door, Maren-Kristine Haug-Larsen came breezing in. "I have to go home after the children's program on TV," she said, and disappeared like a shadow into the closet.

Maren-Kristine is six years old and Kara's best friend on earth. Her hair is long, almost white, and she looks like an angel, a glossy magazine angel. But that's only on the outside. If an old lady mistakes her for one of the glossy magazine angels, bends down toward her, and asks in a sweet old-lady voice, "And what's your name, my dear?" Maren-Kristine spits, aiming close to her right shoe, always hitting where she aims, looks at the old lady, and says, "And wouldn't you like to know?"

No old lady ever asks twice.

T H R E E

Einar lives with his grandparents. His mother and father died in a car accident four years ago. About two years after that he came to Veitvet. It's been two years since he moved to the desk behind mine, where he was immediately hidden by me. Even though he's older he doesn't stand very high above sea level. The desk behind mine is a nice place to sleep totally undisturbed. Miss Monsen, our teacher last year, sometimes thought he wasn't even at school. If he puts his mind to it, Einar can be invisible.

He never talks about his life before he came here, not about his parents, not about the place he used to live, or about his old friends. Not one word. The little I know, Mum's told me, and she knows only what she learned from someone who's an acquaintance of his grandparents.

Apart from being good at sleeping behind my back, Einar is a terrific belcher. So am I, so we quickly became great friends. He comes over to my place every day, and when he leaves he always forgets something: a shoe or even both his shoes, his jacket, a sweater. One time he even forgot his trousers. He was wearing a bathing suit. I guess most people would call him forgetful. At first I thought it was strange that he has such a short memory, not even to notice he's wearing only one shoe. And there I'd be, shouting out the window, "Einar, you forgot your shoe!" But he'd simply smile and wave, calling out, "I'll get it tomorrow," before he ran home. He'd come back the next day, get his shoe, and leave something else. I stopped calling after him a long time ago. I got used to him leaving things.

"Einar 'forgets' things so he has an excuse to come back," Mum said the time I was leaning out the window, waving his trousers.

"But he can come here any time he wants," I said, a bit confused.

"Maybe he doesn't dare believe that," she said.

I really think she was right. I don't know if Einar is ever going to believe it. But in the meantime he comes by every day, as regularly as clockwork, and we're all used to him now.

When Mum opens the door for him in the morning, she hands him his socks, or whatever he left behind the night before, just as naturally as she says, "Hello, Einar. Go right in and wake him up. I've been trying to get him up for ages. Maybe you'll have better luck."

And he does.

"Set your alarm clock for a quarter to five tomorrow morning," Einar said one evening a couple of days later. I just stared at him.

"We'll take a trip downtown before the city wakes up. There's nothing like a deserted city. The streets seem bigger and broader early in the morning before all the people arrive. Come and see for yourself."

"Do you go downtown in the middle of the night?" The idea seemed crazy to me.

"In the early morning, not in the night. And now in the summer it's light, and it's so empty you can walk right down the middle of Karl Johan if you want to, and there's nobody around to care. No traffic, nothing. Well, almost."

"Do you do that often?"

"As often as I can and when I have money for the subway."

"But your grandparents, don't they notice you're gone?"

"Not always. They don't hear too well. And if they're awake when I get back, I don't tell them I've been downtown."

I looked at him. Einar is a mystery to me. We've been friends for two years, but he has a lot of secrets.

"Don't you get tired during the day?" I wondered.

"You bet." Einar laughed. "Why do you think I sleep at school? Are you coming or what? We can go to the lake afterward, to swim, or just hang around for the rest of the day."

"Of course I'm coming," I said. "You'll be outside my place a little before five tomorrow morning?"

"At ten to," Einar said.

I could hardly wait.

I felt more dead than alive at a quarter to five the next morning when the alarm went off. I checked my impulse to throw the clock at the wall when I remembered why I was getting up so early.

I dressed in a hurry and looked out the window. Einar was already there. I waved to him, holding out the T-shirt he'd forgotten the night before. He shook his head. He wouldn't be needing it for our trip. Standing quite still, I looked around me, thinking. Keys? Yes, there they were. And money? Yes. I found a piece of paper and wrote a note saying I was taking an early morning walk with Einar, left the message on the chest of drawers in the hall, and went out without making a sound.

The morning sun was yellow above the shopping center. The whole world was asleep, except the woman who sold subway tickets. Einar greeted her like an old friend.

"Good morning, boys. You're up early, and not even crying."

We chuckled. "You're not crying either," Einar said.

The ticket woman smiled and wished us a pleasant journey.

"She's okay," Einar said as we walked up the steps to the platform. The sun hadn't been up very long, but it was warm. We sat on a bench to wait. The station is built so that the platform is the same height as the roofs of the surrounding buildings, and it gives you the feeling of sitting high up in the sky with all the world beneath you.

I looked down at Beverveien and the house where the new family had moved in. The windows glowed like newly polished brass kettles from Toten. I had passed the house several times in the last couple of days but hadn't seen any of the children. The grown-ups seemed to be redecorating the flat.

Just Einar and I stood on the platform. I had this funny feeling something was missing. It took some time to figure out what it was: the sounds. There was a strange silence, a totally unfamiliar silence, and in it was a wasp, buzzing on the corner by the stairs.

"Good, eh?" Einar asked.

"Mmmmn." All of a sudden I understood why he sneaked out in the early morning hours while everyone else was in bed, catching the last dreams before waking.

The tracks started singing, then the train came. There was no fighting to get on board; only Einar and I got on. We sat down in the back seat of the last car. Apart from a man sleeping with his mouth wide open some seats ahead, the car was empty.

Einar never talks much, which I like. I

looked around and enjoyed the silence. The train stopped and started at all the usual stations, but no one shouted, swore, or laughed out loud, and it felt strange.

Outside, the houses were asleep in the early morning light. The world was green and yellow until the driver announced, "Watch the doors!" and the train dived into the tunnel at Hasle station. The wheels squeaked noisily through the underground darkness until we were asked to leave the train at Sentrum station — the last and wettest station on the line because the roof leaks.

There were puddles of water and mosquitoes on the platform, and a steep escalator heading up into the daylight.

F O U R

THREE GRAY PIGEONS were tripping around, searching for food in the street when we came up. If they could eat garbage they'd grow fat in no time. There was trash all over. It rustled and moved in the wind. We began our journey up Karl Johan to the castle, with our usual two short and one long belch, and followed the yellow line in the middle of the street until we reached the Grand Hotel. We had a narrow escape when a newspaper van came shrieking to a halt beside us. Only a giant leap onto the sidewalk saved us. Two big packs of newspapers were thrown out in front of the kiosk, then the van went off, the litter stirring behind it. Einar and I looked at each other. Dangerous town, this, even when asleep. We moved on.

A well-dressed couple came walking toward us on rather unsteady legs. "Taxi!" they called, but there were no taxis around.

"Why couldn't we do as I suggested!" the woman shouted very loudly. "Oh no! You always know best, don't you? Why is it no one ever listens to me? No. NEVER!"

The answer to her question is a well-kept secret, even today, because just then a taxi came along, and off they went.

A man was sleeping on the bench in front of the music pavilion. He wasn't easy to spot, and we could hardly see him, but a cruising police car was more than visible. My protests were silenced as Einar hurried us into Universitetsgaten to hide until the car had passed by.

"But we haven't done anything wrong," I whispered.

"I know that, but the police don't," was Einar's answer.

What did he mean by that? I couldn't figure it out, but I did as I was told. We ran until we found a doorway and pressed up against the wall in the semidarkness. The police car didn't bother with us, but stopped beside the man who lay sleeping by the pavilion. That's when I discovered we were not alone in the doorway. There was someone else there. She looked cold and tired, as if she'd been sitting there for a very long time.

"Hi," I said, guessing she was about two or three years older than I.

"Got a smoke?" she asked.

I shook my head. "I don't smoke," I explained.

Her sad eyes viewed me. "No. I didn't think you would. But could you give me some kroner for a cup of coffee? Brrr. It's cold, sleeping out. You can get rheumatism long before you're twenty in this town."

Without thinking, I handed her the money I had in my pocket — a five-kroner coin.

"Thanks, pal. I'll be off, then. See you." She tried to get up, but maybe the rheumatism had already started. Her knees were so stiff she could hardly stand. Were there cafés open this early? I didn't know, but if there were, I was sure she would know.

She got up very, very carefully. Einar had turned away when I started talking to the girl, his shoulders hunched as if he was cold too. She had to get past him to get out to the street. She stopped next to him and stared at him.

23

"Holy smoke! Is that you, Einar? It's been such a long time." She grabbed his right hand and shook it violently, then moved closer and gave him a hug. A hug!

Einar murmured something that sounded like "Hello, Vera," and asked where she was living now.

"Nowhere, as you can see," Vera replied, and in her jeans and pink jacket leaned up against the dark wall next to Einar. Her hair, which she had fastened in a ponytail, was standing straight up. She must have been at least fifteen. And she knew Einar.

"Have you seen the Stenstads lately?"

The question made Einar jump as if someone had hit him in the face. He shook his head and told her not to talk about it. "Be quiet! Don't talk about it!" He kept repeating this as if he was stuttering. Don't talk about it. Don't talk about it.

Don't talk about what? Who was this Vera? And who were the ones with that name she'd asked him about?

"But Einar, where do you live?"

"At Grandma and Grandpa's."

And then he got another hug, and Vera whispered something eagerly in his ear. Afterward she said bye and was gone.

It had never occurred to me that Einar would meet an old friend in a doorway at six o'clock on a Saturday morning, but suddenly everything seemed possible.

"Who was she?" I wondered out loud. The girl had gone and we were left alone in the darkness.

"Someone I used to know. Before."

"Before you moved to Veitvet?"

He gave a nod. "Why did you give her your money?"

I thought for a moment before I answered, "Because she looked as if she was a long way from home."

"Yeah. You're right. A very long way from home." Einar went ahead of me out of the doorway.

The city came back to me out there in the sunshine on the street. It would be another warm day. Einar didn't utter a word but seemed totally absorbed in his thoughts as we walked. Without speaking, we reached the subway station and stopped at the point where Karl Johan starts dropping toward the big railway station that lies close to the harbor and the ships going to Denmark.

Karl Johan, the busiest street in the city, lay quiet, showing no signs of street musicians, vendors of any kind, or men with great and important messages to the human race. I tried to picture the street on a winter's morning but couldn't. Luckily, it was still summer and a long time until Christmas. I decided to ask to come with Einar on other early morning trips. But who was Vera?

Einar found out our train had just left, so we walked to the next station by Jernbanetorget.

There were more people at this station. We went past the flower shop in the house with the slanting glass roof and the big windows. Inside were tall green palm trees. Every time I pass that shop I hope to see a bunch of monkeys inside, jumping from one tree to another. It would fit in so nicely, I think. But no monkeys today, as usual.

We could hear him a long time before we saw him. He came around the bend, and there he was. In a wheelchair, with a blanket on his lap covering his legs, he played the harmonica for the few people who hurried past him. I guessed that the plastic bag on the ground next to the chair contained his lunch. I tried to figure out what song he was playing, but it was impossible.

"Do you know what he's playing?" I asked Einar.

"No use asking me. I could never tell the difference between one song and another. But it doesn't sound too bad, does it?"

"But that's just it," I said excitedly. "Because he isn't playing anything. He's making it up as he goes along, and it sounds pretty good."

I must have spoken louder than I meant to because the man in the wheelchair looked at us and blinked his eyes above the harmonica.

I went on, but not so loud this time. "That's what's so great about the harmonica. You just blow away and pretend you can do it, and it sounds okay. Just imagine! This guy is making his living by not being able to play the harmonica! And nobody has to find out, because they don't have the time to stop and listen. And even if they do stop, they'll just think they don't know the song. Oh, Einar, couldn't you give him the krone you have in your shoe? I think he's a brave man and deserves encouragement. You'll get it back later."

"No, it's okay. I want him to have it." Einar took off his right shoe, got out the coin, hopped across to the man, and put it in the basket on his lap. "Keep on rockin'," Einer said to the man as he stepped back into his shoe. "Boy, I'm such a jerk!" he whispered to me as we rushed

27

away down the corridor. "The man can't walk at all!"

We ran through the turnstile. The Grorud line would be leaving in two minutes. It was time to go home.

F I V E

MONDAY MORNING AT half past ten the summer holidays were officially over. Our class had moved to another room. Apart from that, nothing had changed. No, that wasn't quite true. There was a new boy, one of the pirates from Beverveien. I had thought they were Pakistani, but I was wrong. He came from Afghanistan, and his name was Hewad. He spoke Norwegian quite well. He'd been in the country for nearly three years, living in downtown Tøyen until his family had moved here to Veitvet the week before.

He looked upset when Miss Monsen asked

him if he'd say something in Afghan. He refused. He didn't want to say anything. Miss
Monsen handled it nicely and said it could wait
until we got to know each other better. Hewad
looked relieved. He'd taken the desk next to
Einar's, behind me.

The first day after the holidays we always
write down the new timetable. We were to
have the same old teachers for another year.
The only change was that we'd have Goofy for
gymnastics, and that was definitely good news.
Afterward we all talked about where we'd
spent the summer and what we'd been doing. I
just hated it. I was already dreading the days to
come when the teachers would ask the pupils
what they'd been doing. There aren't many
teachers who tell you what *they* did. Just imagine! Tell the Norwegian teacher *what* you did;
tell your geography teacher *where* you did it;
and tell your English teacher the whole thing
all over again in English. It's incredible what
the teaching profession manages to squeeze out
of a lousy eight-week holiday that passes too
quickly!

I spent the summer at Kapp. It doesn't take
long to tell about it. I go there every year. Einar goes every summer with his grandparents
to the small farm they used to run outside

Skjeberg. Just once I wish Einar could come with me to Kapp, but his grandparents always say no.

We have only one lesson the first day after the holidays, and as we were leaving, I asked Hewad to come out with us. He wouldn't, though. He said he had to hurry home. He was going downtown. Einar looked angry when I asked Hewad along, and was extremely relieved when Hewad said no.

"What's the matter with you?" I asked. "He seems all right, doesn't he?"

"Just leave him alone! Can't you see that's what he wants? He doesn't want to get to know you." Einar must have had a bad night or something. "Oh, hell. Let's forget it. You want to go swimming?"

Hewad was ahead of us, and Einar didn't smile until the dark figure went off down Beverveien.

"Last one up the hill is a sissy!" Einar shouted, and started to run. Einar is as quick as the wind and is always first, even though my legs are much longer than his.

We shared a soft ice at the ice cream parlor before we went to get our bathing suits. Kara and Maren-Kristine were standing on the stairs, talking to Mum, when we got home.

"Why can't you go to Maren-Kristine's place today?" Mum was asking Kara.

Maren-Kristine sighed, and Kara made a face. "No way. It's too dull," Kara said.

"But you can't play here. I'm going to clean the flat, so you two will have to stay away until I'm finished."

"But I don't have to be home until half past four," Maren-Kristine explained happily.

"That's okay with me, but you'll still have to wait outside. No one's coming in until I'm finished," Mum said.

Both girls sighed once more, then they left, stubbornly kicking every step on their way down.

"We're going to the lake for a swim, and I need my swimming stuff." I said it so fast Mum didn't have a chance to send me away too. She smiled at us.

"Hello, you two. How was the first day of school? Awful?"

"Yeah. But we have Goofy for gymnastics this year." Goofy plays professional basketball on a very good team.

"We'll take the bikes," I said, nearly falling head first behind the chair, trying to get hold of my beach towel.

"Be sure to be home in time for dinner. By

the way," Mum said to Einar, "you forgot your football yesterday. Want to take it now?"

"No. I'll get it later. We're playing this afternoon."

Mum laughed and said, "Have a good time."

We met up with Kara and Maren-Kristine again outside.

"It's unfair," Kara said. "We can't go to Maren-Kristine's today because we don't want to paint. We always have to paint at her place. I don't feel like it and you don't either, do you?"

Maren-Kristine most definitely did not want to paint. "No. Today I want to do something quite different, but I don't know what."

Maren-Kristine's mother works part-time at the head office for the play schools in town and knows *all* about children. And what she knows is that the best way for children to express their imagination is in watercolors. I guess that's why Maren-Kristine spends so much time with us, where she's never expected to express anything. It must be very tiring being the daughter of a part-time play school office clerk. Kara and Maren-Kristine agreed a long time ago that they'd go to Maren-Kristine's place only when they really want to paint.

Maren-Kristine comes around every morning

at about nine and announces that she has to be home at half past four. That's her dinnertime. After dinner she comes back, and as she crosses the threshold she announces that she has to be home after the children's program on TV. She has announced her schedule every day for years now, and we all know it by heart.

The water was almost too warm in the small lake. We decided that next time we'd go farther to the large lake a couple of miles away. Einar and I relaxed, lounging underneath our favorite tree a stone's throw from the water. I stared at him from time to time, not quite sure of what I saw. I was getting the idea that I didn't know him as well as I had thought I did. I tried to think of ways to ask him about Vera, but he pretended not to understand my hints.

S I X

I SPEND EVERY summer at Kapp, Østre Toten, with Grandma and Grandpa and Peder and Anna. Peder is Dad's older brother. He took over running the farm from Grandpa and Grandma. I don't think Dad ever wanted to become a farmer. When he finished school he went to Oslo to find a job. Lots of people from Kapp went to Oslo to work in those days. Most of them became construction workers, living in barracks all week, then catching the shuttle bus on Saturday afternoons to go home for a short weekend. Sunday nights they were off again, back to Oslo. After a couple of years on a building site, Dad started working for the railway and now he's an engine driver.

My grandparents still live on the farm, in the old house. Peder and Anna live in the new one. They grow wheat and keep sheep. The sheep are usually grazing way up in the hills at Totenåsen when we come for our holidays, and all we have to do is get the hay in. There's not much work to be done on a farm in the summer, apart from small repairs and painting, things like that.

Anna was a nurse before she and Peder married. She does part-time nursing now, working the night shift at the hospital in Gjøvik. They have two kids, Lars and Maria. Maria is a year and a half older than Kara, and Lars is two years older than I. But we never worry about the difference in our ages. We've known each other forever.

I never get tired of Kapp. I wouldn't want to go anywhere else. There used to be a ferry from Hamar to Kapp, but now there's only the old quay to remind us of it.

We bought our first car just a few years ago, when Kara was a baby. Before that, we went by train to Kapp. We had to change trains at Eina, and that gave us time for an ice cream before we went on to Gjøvik, where Peder always waited for us at the station.

I liked going by train, but the best part was

watching Dad. The moment we left Eina he became a totally different person. He relaxed, laughed — and loud, too — then he began to speak the Kapp dialect. Dad never speaks it at home.

Grandpa says he doesn't care where he lives in this world as long as he can look out the window and see Mjøsa. That's when Dad's face gets this strange expression, and I think that deep down he feels that way too. Because every time we're getting near Mjøsa, the largest lake in Norway, Dad changes.

These days we go by car, and the change in him starts at Eidsvoll. When we turn left near Minnesund and drive along the foot of the Totenåsen hills, no earthly power could stop him. He has to tell us all the stories about when he was a little boy at Kapp. There's no use telling him we've heard the stories at least five hundred times before. Even so, we nearly choke to death laughing and beg him to stop, but he never will. He goes on and on with his stories until we arrive at the doorstep.

Mum's from Drammen, and such things never happen when we drive there.

This last summer was like any other. Nothing to write home about, least of all a school composition. Dad's vacation started at the beginning of July, and we drove off immediately after having stuffed the car to the limit. We hadn't been driving more than twenty minutes when we heard a terrible noise.

"That car is making a horrible noise," Dad shouted, pointing at the car ahead of us. "There ought to be a law against rattletraps like that."

"But maybe it's our car," Mum said. "Are you quite sure it isn't?"

That made him lose his temper. "No way. There's nothing wrong with this car, nothing at all. It's seven years old but good as new."

We went on, and so did the racket.

"Dad, I really think it's our car!" I had to shout to make myself heard.

I couldn't hear his answer, but he stopped the car at the side of the road. The noise also stopped.

Mum and Dad got out. Kara and I did too. There we were on the side of the motorway with all four of us down on our knees, looking under the car, the traffic booming past. Kara and I were ordered back into the car. I sat down in the doorway.

"I can't find anything wrong," Dad said. "It must have been the car ahead of us, as I told you."

"No." Mum was firm. "It's definitely something wrong with *this* car. Try rocking it a bit, Harald."

Dad pushed up and down on the left fender.

"Something's loose." Mum looked a bit worried.

"Can't be," Dad said. He'd said that heaven knows how many times in the last quarter of an hour.

"Look for yourself." Now it was Mum's turn to push on the fender.

Something was loose all right. The exhaust pipe was broken, right underneath the engine. There was no way Dad could deny it any longer.

"We'll have to do something about that," he declared.

It was close to four on a Friday afternoon. Everyone hurried back into the car.

"Let's see if we can find a gas station with a mechanic," Mum suggested.

The car started with a wild roar, and off we went. We left the motorway at the next exit and soon found a gas station. It was now five after four.

"Come right in," a friendly man said, and then he vanished into the well underneath the car. "I can fasten it for you so it'll keep still," he told Dad. "It won't help the noise, but the exhaust won't fall off." He fastened the pipe in no time, and didn't even want any money.

Dad started telling his childhood stories the moment we passed Eidsvoll, and even though we could hardly hear a word of what he was saying, we nearly died laughing.

S E V E N

TUESDAY MORNING Maren-Kristine slipped in as I opened the front door on my way to school. She looked at me, about to say something.

"You have to be home at half past four," I said, before she had a chance to speak.

Maren-Kristine looked at me in great surprise. "How on earth did you know?"

I didn't want to reveal this secret, and raced down the stairs in long leaps.

Einar was waiting for me under the subway overpass as usual. We crossed Veitvetveien below the shopping center and stole a couple of yellow plums each. The plum tree was just inside the fence, and the plums were almost ripe.

A bit farther down the road Hewad appeared. He was with an older boy — I'm sure it was his brother. Einar had to stop to tie his shoelaces, and I looked around, waiting. Lots of people were going down the hill this morning; school had started for real. The holidays were definitely over, and Einar and I were in grade six.

Einar tied his other shoelace too, even though it wasn't undone. "Just to make sure," he said.

Einar and I, we're always together. I can't remember the last time we quarreled. I guess we never have, and not until these last few days did I notice that he'd been keeping things from me.

"Have you seen Vera lately?" The question jumped from my mouth. I didn't even have time to think before it was out.

His suntanned neck stiffened for a second, then his shoelace was undone again, but his voice was quite calm when he answered, "No."

"Have you been downtown lately?"

"No."

"Why can't you tell me about her?" I asked.

"What do you want to know?" Slowly and quietly he tied his shoelace once more, threw a quick glance downhill, and so did I. Hewad and his brother were out of sight. "What do you want to know?" He repeated the question with a voice much calmer than his eyes. I was torturing him, sticking a knife into him. Behind his poker face I saw I was hurting him, but I couldn't stop. I *had* to know. He *had* to tell me about Vera. It was as if Vera had become the most important thing in my life. I couldn't live another day unless I knew about her.

"Everything," I answered.

"I got to know her at a place I used to live. She's from Mosjøen originally."

"You can't tell from her accent."

"No. She hasn't been home in a long time," he said.

"Why hasn't she been home in a long time?"

"She didn't like it there, so she ran away."

"How?"

"By train."

"Train?" I was starting to feel stupid. Was he pulling my leg? No. It didn't seem like it. But he'd made me terribly curious.

"Yes, by train. She hid in the toilet when the conductor came. If you don't lock the door, you know, he might think there's no one in there. She never had the money to buy a ticket. Sometimes she managed to get all the way to Trondheim before she was found and sent home again. When she managed to get to Oslo, it took them longer to find her."

"*They?*"

Einar didn't answer, just looked at me, his face a stiff mask. "You've never had to pay for a ticket, have you?" he asked me.

That's what you get when your dad's an engine driver.

Suddenly I felt awful, as if everything was all my fault: my fault Vera had run away from home; my fault that in his past Einar had known a dark and mysterious girl.

Einar started walking downhill. His back told me he wouldn't say one more word about Vera. He was hurrying, and I ran after him.

Vera.

I could picture a little girl stealing onto the train, hiding in the toilet, pressing her thin body against the wall behind the door as the conductor passed by in the corridor outside. She'd managed to get all the way to Oslo without a ticket, and "they" had not managed to get hold of her. Who were "they"? They had captured her in the end and sent her to the place where Einar had met her. Where?

Einar slowed down at last and turned toward me, smiling in his old usual way. "Hurry up, or we'll be late."

"That's because you had to tie your shoe-laces several hundred times," I said, and Einar grinned.

Then we gave out with two short and one long belch. And then, just to show we really meant it, we did it again.

E I G H T

W HEN EINAR HAS religious instruction, I
have an ethical culture class. It's the only time
Einar and I are not together at school. This
year I would have ethical culture every Tuesday and Friday. It turned out that Hewad was
taking ethical culture, too.

Last year we learned a lot about the Gypsies.
I didn't know until then that Hitler disliked
Gypsies as much as he did Jews, and that's why
there are so few of them left in Europe. We had
a visit by a woman from the office dealing with
Gypsy affairs, and she told us a bit about what
it's like to be a Gypsy in Norway today.

What I'd really like to do is travel — like

the Gypsies. Around the world. Experience strange and mysterious things. See what life is like on the other side of the world. It's got to be very different from here. You can read about it and look at pictures, but that's not enough. I want to see it all for myself. I want to feel the desert sand in my eyes when the sandstorms are raging through the Sahara. I want to swim in the Ganges River, climb the Himalayas, feel the earth shake in Japan, and I want to go to Mexico. For a start.

In earlier days there were people called globetrotters. They traveled everywhere they wanted in this whole wide world. I bet they were rich, and even though I'm not, maybe I could become a sailor? A pirate? A Gypsy?

Counting Hewad, there were twelve of us in the ethical culture class — five girls and seven boys.

When our teacher, Leif Bøe — Loafy, for short — asked Hewad if he would say something in Afghan, Hewad was all smiles. He said good morning in a completely unintelligible tongue. But that was all we got. Maybe I could learn some Afghan. It sounded awfully difficult, but would come in very handy when I started traveling.

Hewad told us that his family had been

forced to flee Kabul right after the Soviet invasion of December 27, 1979. Uncles, aunts, and cousins, they all had to leave. They had gone to Peshawar in Pakistan where large refugee camps were springing up. One of his uncles had gone to England, the other had stayed in Peshawar. Several times a year the uncle who now lived in Pakistan would go back into Afghanistan to buy carpets, which he then sold in Peshawar. There were no jobs for Afghan refugees in Peshawar.

Hewad's father had been a journalist on a daily newspaper in Kabul. One of the first things the Soviets had done was to take control of the newspapers and radio. Hewad's family managed to get out in time, and after some months in the camp, they had come to Norway. Since then, his father had been cleaning office buildings, but he'd just got a job as a journalist again, which was why they'd moved to Veitvet. But Hewad liked Tøyen better.

Loafy asked him if he often thought about his homeland. Hewad turned away and looked out the window for a while before answering that he thought about it all the time. I followed his gaze. The world outside was as green and bright as any Norwegian summer day. I felt sure there was nothing out there to remind him of the country he'd come from. And that made me think of Grandma and Grandpa at Kapp.

I tried to picture alien soldiers storming the farm at Østre Toten, driving Grandma and Grandpa away. The very idea was impossible because I'd always thought of them as having grown right out of the earth at Kapp, and no living force could ever get them away from there. Maybe Hewad had thought the same about Kabul. What if someone were to come and chase me out of my room on the third floor? What if Mum and Dad and Kara and I all had to run away across the border, across many borders? The thought ended nowhere. I couldn't imagine it. But it had happened to Hewad.

Loafy asked him how he liked Norway.

"It's okay."

I bet he just said that to be polite. I didn't think he liked it here, not much, anyway. But I decided then and there that I would go to Afghanistan after the war ended and the country was free again. I could visit Hewad . . .

Hewad and Loafy talked as old friends, and when the class was over Loafy made him say goodbye in Afghan. I realized that I'd have to learn a lot of languages if I was going to become a globetrotter. As we were leaving I heard

Loafy ask Hewad if he'd bring along something that was typically Afghan to show us. Hewad smiled and said he might bring some food.

When we got near the other kids, Hewad was as uncommunicative as ever. He gave short, evasive answers to my questions, and finally I had to give up. After the last class, he ran off. Einar had also been unusually silent during the afternoon and now he looked very gloomy.

We went out together, but his face was locked up like a bank vault, and just as hard to get into. He said he had to go right home to help his grandmother air the carpets. It didn't seem to bother him. He looked almost pleased when he told me. What in the world had made everyone so moody all of a sudden? First there was Hewad. And now Einar. Was my breath bad or my soap wrong? Were they all going crazy, and right at the beginning of the school year?

I went home and shut myself in my room, listened to music, and *did not* start to work on my composition, "Something Funny Happened to Me on My Summer Holiday." That's the assignment we got. Every year the same dumb assignment. Help!

N I N E

THE NEXT DAY I spent a long time trying to
cheer up Einar. For the first few classes at
school he refused to talk at all, and in the breaks
he just vanished.

"Go talk to Hewad, if you want to." Oh, was
he moody!

"Talk about what?" I asked, but never got an
answer. "I'm not allowed to talk to him, is that
what you mean?"

Einar merely shrugged, not even bothering
to reply.

Not until after the fourth class did he come
up to me with a cautious smile, poking my back,
saying, "Hi, Jonas."

"Two short and a long one?" I asked. Then we laughed and belched two short and a long one so many times that we didn't have any breath left, and rolled on the ground laughing hysterically. Then everything was all right again. Thank heaven. I couldn't imagine how to get along without Einar.

Kara and Maren-Kristine had also had a busy day. Dad and I were told all about it during our dinner of meatloaf. Mum told the story and Kara supplied additional comments from the little kids' side of the table.

Maren-Kristine had come as usual around nine while Kara was having her breakfast, and both of them had settled down in the kitchen.

"It was my day to do the laundry," Mum went on. "And I was up and down to the cellar all day. I completely forgot about Kara and Maren-Kristine. I was quite sure they'd gone out, because everything was so quiet."

"Still waters run deep," I mumbled into my meatloaf.

Mum looked at me and nodded. "Right you are," she said. "That's exactly what I discovered when I came up to make myself a cup of tea. Eight pounds of sugar was spread over the kitchen floor. Eight pounds of crunchy granulated sugar. The sugar bags stood like worn-out boots on the bench. It was as if a snowstorm had blown through the room."

"We were feeding the chickens," Kara explained.

"The chickens?" asked Dad.

"Yes, the chickens. We were feeding them, and I can tell you they were mighty hungry."

Dad didn't give the impression of having understood, so Kara went on with her explanation. "You just pretend that you're in a hen house and that you have chicken food in the bags. You throw it around, saying, 'Here, chickie, chickie!' It was only a game, you see."

"That's when I gave them a broom each and told them to play the I'm-cleaning-the-kitchen-floor game. Then I threw them out," Mum said.

"And that was a stroke of luck because it was such a great day for watercolors, you can't imagine. But first we bought some Hubba Bubba." Kara cast me a quick glance, but I didn't say anything.

Both girls have a well-developed talent for business and are seldom short of money for bubble gum. We never talk about it at home, not even to Mum. She wouldn't understand, Kara says, and I guess she's right.

Maren-Kristine has eyes like a falcon and can spot an empty bottle however high the grass around it might be. Just a glint in the sun, and Maren-Kristine is right there to grab it.

And Kara sings.

The best time for singing is when the Undergrounders are coming home. She has her favorite place outside the station, and sings a lot of hit songs in both Norwegian and Swedish. She also has some old standards, like "In a Hospital Ward," for those who have passed the halfway point in life. Kara has a song for every occasion. But not when Dad's on his way home. Then she takes off in a hurry. It's bad for business to be scolded publicly, so she takes a break when Dad is due home.

She sings so beautifully that the grown-ups stop and listen, smiling. And the fact that Maren-Kristine is collecting the money is also good for profit. Everything they get is spent on Hubba Bubba. And if the day has been more than usually good, the surplus is hidden in Kara's closet. No chewing gum is allowed to enter the home of Maren-Kristine. If it does, it goes right into the garbage.

"Maren-Kristine showed me how to mix mauve paint, and we painted mauve horses for hours," Kara said. "Afterward we had sandwiches and lemonade, and then we painted some more horses. After today we don't have to paint for years because we have no imagination left." Kara looked very pleased with herself.

Maren-Kristine rang the doorbell right after dinner, but she wouldn't come in, even though Mum said she could.

"I'd rather go out anyway," said Kara.

"Keep away from the trash containers!" Mum shouted after them as they skipped off down the stairs.

T E N

EINAR CAME. He'd forgotten his schoolbag when he went home for dinner earlier, and we decided to do our math homework before going out. It didn't take long.

This was, as I mentioned before, the year when every flat at Veitvet was getting a balcony, and carpenters were busy everywhere. There was a trash container outside number five. Old windows and woodwork had been dumped into it, and it looked like the masts of a shipwreck at the bottom of the sea. The container was overflowing. And up there, on the top, was Maren-Kristine Haug-Larsen.

When Einar and I approached, Kara came out from behind the big container.

"Look what we found!" she cried, and raised her arms high, holding something gray that must once have been white. It was a rag doll. It was old and worn, with no clothes and no eyes, only long black woolen hair and a red, smiling mouth.

"A sleeping doll." Kara held it, studying it closely. The doll was as big as a real baby.

Maren-Kristine jumped down from the top of the trash bin and landed right next to me. "I know what we'll do," she said. "Do you have any paper?"

I said I didn't, but Einar found a notebook in his bag and tore out a page.

Maren-Kristine thanked him and said she had her own pencil. "We're going to write a letter to the Witch," she declared. Then she and Kara sat down on the steps.

"But what are you going to say?" Kara was more than curious.

"I'm going to say that Dolly has no home, and that the Witch must take care of her." Maren-Kristine chewed her pencil.

"You are so clever," said Kara admiringly.

Maren-Kristine agreed, and started to write.

Einar and I sat down on the grass a little ways off. We decided to wait and see what would happen. The Witch lives on the fourth floor of our building, and no one has ever seen her go out during the day. This could be exciting.

The two girls went inside carrying the doll and the letter. Einar and I lay on the lawn, chewing on long blades of grass. Hardly a minute had passed before the girls came rushing out, right into the arms of Sørensen, the super, who was just passing with a box of bulbs.

"Oh, it's you!" said Kara.

"Good," said Maren-Kristine. "We've lost something down the garbage chute."

"But you don't live here," said Sørensen.

"No, but we've lost something down the chute," Maren-Kristine repeated. She can be very persistent.

"Okay, okay, we'll have a look then," Sørensen said, and gave the girls a friendly smile as he opened the door to the incinerator room. There was Dolly, sitting on a shopping bag next to two milk cartons and a heap of carrot peel.

"There she is!" Maren-Kristine cried, pointing.

"You'll have to take better care of her from now on," Sørensen said. He fetched the doll and gave it to Maren-Kristine. Then he locked the door and went off.

Kara curtsied and said, "Many thanks." Maren-Kristine said nothing until Sørensen had gone. Then she said, "We have to try again."

"What happened?" asked Einar. "And how did the doll end up in the garbage chute?"

Kara giggled. "We put the doll on the mat outside the Witch's door, with the letter on her stomach. Then we rang the doorbell and ran. The Witch opened the door, then a minute later we heard two bangs."

"It was the second bang that did it. I knew something was wrong," said Maren-Kristine. "And I was right. Now we have to write another letter, because the Witch kept the first one."

Einar took out his notebook again and gave Maren-Kristine another page.

"We can help you with the letter, if you want," I suggested.

Maren-Kristine had to think about this proposition for quite a while. Then she gave me the piece of paper and said, "Start like this: 'Dear Madam, I am a very unhappy foundling without a home.'"

I nodded and started to write. Then I happened to look at the doll that lay facedown on the grass, and had to laugh. Einar was sitting beside the doll.

Maren-Kristine went on, just as serious as before. " 'Dear Madam.' "

"Again?" I asked.

"Be quiet. I have to think. 'Dear Madam, Please let me stay with you. Don't throw me out a second time.' Then sign it 'Dolly,' because that's her name."

"The Witch's name?" asked Einar.

"No. The doll's," Maren-Kristine explained, then declared that the letter was finished.

"Good luck, Dolly," Kara whispered, and kissed the doll's pale, dirty cheek before the two girls went once more into number five.

Einar and I sat down behind a car to wait. I threw a quick glance at the kitchen window four floors up, and thought I caught a glimpse of a face, just for a second, but then it was gone. Was the Witch prepared for the next attack by the homeless Dolly? Time would tell. The adoption plan was under way, with expert help from Kara Bakken and Maren-Kristine Haug-Larsen.

This time, they came out even faster.

"She opened the door the moment we rang the bell," Kara gasped. "Did we run! Holy smoke, was I ever scared!"

"But there was only one bang," said Maren-Kristine. "Maybe one of you could go up to see if the doll's still there," she said to me and Einar.

"Up there? To the Witch? Are you nuts?" I asked. "What if she comes out and turns me into a frog?"

Maren-Kristine shook her head and explained in a very adult tone that the chances were rather slim, as that could only happen to a real prince.

I let myself be persuaded to go up to the fourth floor. Before I went, I threw another quick glance up at the windows, but now they stared at me, empty and blind. Then I raced upstairs, two steps at a time like a silent panther. There was no one around on the fourth floor, either beast or human — or doll. The sign on the Witch's door told me her name was Evelyn Hansen. Her door was shut. There was no sign of Dolly. The only thing for me to do was to go back the way I'd come. So I did.

"The doll's gone. The Witch must have taken her," I reported when I rejoined the others.

"Maybe the Witch will let her stay this time," Kara said with a hopeful expression.

"That, I fear, we shall never know," answered Maren-Kristine gloomily.

E L E V E N

I SPENT THE whole of Saturday morning lying on my bed, staring at the ceiling. Mum had told me to stay in my room until I had written at least part of the composition about the summer holidays.

Kapp is my second home. We have our own apartment in the attic in Anna and Peder's house. It's even bigger than the one here at Veitvet, and Kara has her own room. Even Mum has a room of her own, a tiny place where she keeps her drawing materials. She does most of her drawing out of doors and takes her sketchbook, pencils, and charcoal sticks everywhere, so she always has dirty hands.

This summer Mum did a great drawing of Kara and our cousin Maria. Anna said Mum should try to get it in an exhibition, but Mum said fiddlesticks. There were too many artists already and, aside from that, what she really liked best was to make things in clay. So Anna got the drawing and Peder framed it and now it's hanging on the living room wall at Kapp.

I spend a lot of time when I'm there in the old house with Grandma and Grandpa. Granny knows all kinds of stories about pirates, and each year she makes up new ones. Granny is the only one who calls Kara by her real name, Katarina. I think that's because Kara is named after her mother, my great-grandmother, whom I've only ever seen in a picture. She's there behind glass on the living room wall — Katarina the first, that is — looking very solemn. Granny says Katarina's only twenty-five in that picture, but if you ask me, I'd say she's at least fifty, considering the hairdo.

Dad and my uncle Peder are not much alike, but their voices are. When we're at Kapp it's hard to tell them apart. At home Dad talks as they do in Oslo, but at Kapp he speaks the local dialect. I once asked him why he switches dialects, and he said he'd got used to doing it automatically. But that wasn't quite true because when he was a young boy, working as a bricklayer's assistant and living all week in a barracks in Oslo, the others teased him because he couldn't speak proper Norwegian. Granny told me that. Proper Norwegian!

I spend most of the time at Kapp with my cousin Lars. When we're not playing football, or on the beach, we borrow Peder's boat and go fishing or swimming. It's a good way to get rid of Kara and Maria because they're not allowed onboard unless there are grown-ups along.

I could almost hear the waves against the boat as I lay on my bed in the third-floor room to the right. But summer was over, and school had started, and I wasn't staying indoors one minute longer. I was sure Einar would be back by now from his shopping trip downtown with his grandmother, and I wanted to go over and find out.

When I was outside number five, I heard someone say, "Pssst," but when I looked around I couldn't see anyone. I heard the sound again, this time followed by, "You, boy!" I looked around again, but still couldn't see anyone. Then I realized that I was the boy someone was psssting at. I looked up.

Leaning out her kitchen window, four floors

up, was the Witch. It couldn't have been anyone but her. I thought she must be out to have
her revenge, and my heart went down to my
shoes.

"You, boy, come up here," the Witch called
to me. And smiled!

"Me?" I asked, a little stupidly.

"Yes, you," the Witch replied, and shut the
window.

I didn't want to go upstairs and wished that
Einar was with me. But to prove I was no
chicken, I went up the stairs and rang the doorbell of Evelyn Hansen.

The door opened, and there she was. Maybe
she was a hundred years old. She was no more
than four feet tall, in a long red dress down to
her ankles, with no shoes on. Her hair was
short and steel gray, standing straight out like
porcupine quills.

I longed to turn around and say, sorry, maybe
some other time, but I went in and shut the
door behind me.

The hall was in semidarkness.

"I've often seen you outside," the Witch began, "with a light-haired boy."

"Yes, Einar," I mumbled while I started taking off my sneakers.

"No, keep them on," the Witch said. "I want to ask you to do some shopping for me. My back is hurting terribly today."

By now we'd entered the living room, where I stopped dead, staring at something sitting on the sofa. Dolly! It really was she, even though she was hard to recognize. She wore a new red-checked dress, had new brown eyes, and looked considerably cleaner than the last time I'd seen her.

The Witch followed my gaze and laughed. A creepy laugh. "That's Dolly. But you know that, don't you? You've met before, haven't you? She rang the doorbell one day and asked to be let in."

I felt my face redden and turned away. I was going to have to tell Kara and Maren-Kristine about this.

"Here's a list of the things I need. You'll go, won't you?"

I took the piece of paper and slowly read the ornate handwriting.

"I can't buy cigarettes. I'm not old enough."

"Then I'll ask my neighbor to buy the cigarettes," the Witch replied, and gave me seventy kroner. The list wasn't a very long one.

"Take care you get seedless grapes. If they haven't got them, don't buy any grapes. I don't

66

like the ones with seeds. They always get stuck in my teeth." The Witch laughed with her mouth wide open, as if she'd told a big joke. I could see there weren't many places for grape seeds to get stuck.

It was too late to say no. I accepted the money, then rushed out to do the fastest shopping of my life.

Totally out of breath, I tumbled up the stairs and rang Evelyn Hansen's doorbell for the second time that day. I carried the plastic bag into the kitchen for her and would have escaped right away if she hadn't grabbed hold of my arm.

"Not so fast! You have to have something for your trouble."

She gave me ten kroner. I thanked her and put it in my pocket as I opened the door. I was about to leave when she stopped me a second time.

"I'm not really a witch, you know," she said, looking me straight in the eyes. "At least not on weekdays."

And with her chuckle ringing in my ears, I got out at last. My hair, as the books say, was standing on end.

Luckily, Einar was home when I got there.

T W E L V E

THIS SATURDAY WAS as warm and sunny as
every other day had been for the last two
months. Even though my visit to the Witch had
been scary, it was over now, and Einar was very
interested when I told him about it.

"Do you really think she's a witch?" he asked
when I'd finished.

"I wouldn't put it past her," I said. "Maybe
she's really three hundred years old. But her
flat was quite ordinary. Old-fashioned but
quite nice, actually. And she didn't have a cat.
Witches always have cats, don't they? Or a ra-
ven?"

I was thinking of fairy tales I'd read, but I

couldn't make it all add up to Evelyn Hansen, however much I tried.

"Of course she's not a witch. That's only for kids," I finally said, smiling. "She gave me ten kroner. Want to go to the swimming pool at Tøyen?"

We agreed to meet by the subway station as soon as we could, and I ran home to get my bathing suit.

The swimming pools and the grass around them were totally packed. We finally found a place to put our towels, way up the hill, but it didn't matter much since we spent most of our time in the water.

In the diving pool, I heard someone call my name. I looked around and saw Hewad in a crowd of suntanned bodies. He was sitting with five or six boys that I guessed were countrymen of his.

"Hewad, hi!" I shouted.

Einar didn't say anything.

"Come and join us," Hewad said, indicating the place they had on the grass right near the pool. I was a bit surprised, but glad, and said yes, we'd like to. Einar went to get our things while I got out of the pool and walked over to the gang.

"He's in my class," Hewad explained to his

friends, who all gave me friendly smiles. And for my sake, they began talking in Norwegian.

It wasn't until then that I remembered that Hewad had told us his family had lived at Tøyen before moving to Veitvet. These must have been his friends from Tøyen. When I asked, it turned out that only one of them actually lived there, but they met often. They explained to me that Afghans abroad tend to keep in close touch.

Einar joined us and sat down carefully at the edge of the circle. He said he wanted to go down to the big pool to swim, so I went with him. As usual, Einar won all our races.

Catching our breath after the last race, I decided it was time to tell Einar a little about Hewad. Up till then, only Loafy had gotten him to talk about himself. Einar and the others who took religion at school hadn't heard any of it because they didn't take Loafy's class.

I tried to explain to Einar what it must feel like to be driven away from your home, to be unable to go back even if you wanted to. I told him how I felt about the farm at Kapp, and Granny and —

"I understand all that perfectly well," Einar said, cutting me short. Then he slid off the edge of the pool and let himself be swallowed

70

by the water. He was under for so long I began to get frightened.

"Are you thinking about Vera?" I asked when he finally broke the blue-clear surface, his face red.

"Vera? No."

He sat beside me on the edge again. "Sometimes, Jonas, you're so stupid I can't stand to see your ugly face." He shoved me roughly into the water.

I had red marks on my arm long after from his fingers. Splash. Into the water. I was so astounded that I swallowed at least a gallon of chlorinated water, and took a long time coughing it up while tears streamed down my face. I barely saw Einar, a dogged expression on his face, running past me with his towel under his arm, on his way out.

I didn't understand.

Had I said something wrong? Was he angry because I'd asked about Vera? Why this sudden outburst? But if you never ask, you never get any answers, do you?

He was behaving very strangely.

I went up to the others and found out they didn't know anything either. Einar had just galloped off like a runaway horse. For a while I wondered what to do. Should I stay, or should

71

I try to catch up with him? I decided to stay. Later, when it was time to go home, Hewad and I took the subway together.

I went to Einar's house right after dinner, but his grandmother said he wasn't home.

"I thought he was with you," she said. I could only shake my head at this.

Einar's grandmother is a stern old lady with lots of white curls. Strict but always kind. And very particular about time: time for school, time for dinner, time for getting home in the evening. But she has kind eyes, and Einar never complains.

I didn't see Einar again that Saturday, and it felt strange. I watched TV with the rest of my family. Not Dad, though, because he was driving a train this weekend. Mum found one of Einar's sneakers he'd left behind. That made me smile. And all of a sudden I felt sure Einar would be back.

T H I R T E E N

V ERY EARLY SUNDAY morning there was a
rattling noise at my window. Clink, clank. In
my half-sleep I thought it was a mosquito
bumping against my window, eager to get in.
Buzz off. You won't get in here, I thought
stupidly.

But there seemed to be more than one mosquito. The clattering and rattling went on, and
I finally had to get up and go to the window —
which was already open — to find out who
wanted to get in so badly.

There was nobody outside, but when I
looked down I saw Einar's white hair and
his arms signaling to me to come down. He

pointed to a plastic bag on the ground beside him and urgently waved at me some more. Then he lifted his right foot, and I could see the white stripes of his sneaker. Next he lifted his left foot until he fell over and wriggled his bare toes. Message received. I grabbed the shoe Mum had found the night before, showed it to him, and threw it out the window, saying I was coming down too, but preferred leaving by the stairs. He understood.

I dressed in a jiffy, even though I had to search for my trousers, which had fallen behind the chair heaped with the clean clothes Mum had told me to put away the day before. There's a time and a place for everything, I told myself, ignoring the clothes. I paused in the hall, listening, but could hear only sounds of sleep. At this time of morning, even Kara was absolutely quiet. She was breathing lightly behind the curtain, and I could hear and feel right to my bones what a peaceful Sunday morning it was. By now I was wide awake. It was not yet half past four as I tiptoed down the stairs on my rubber soles.

Einar was waiting for me on the bench outside, wearing both of his sneakers.

"Hi," I said. "You're up early."

"So are you."

And we went right into the sun, which was already over the roof of the shopping center. The subway station was closed. Only Einar, the birds, and I were awake.

"Let's go to the fields," Einar said, and I agreed, glad to be along on another of Einar's early morning tours. Now things were back to normal.

The Bredtvet Fields are like a wilderness between Veitvet and Kalbakken, overgrown by tall grass, wild flowers, and small trees growing in clumps. You can find yourself a place in the tall grass, sit down, and become invisible to the rest of the world. The sun wasn't warm yet, but it was making an effort.

One after the other, Einar leading, we went down Veitvetveien, along Rådyrveien, crossed the bridge over the brook, and then walked up the path toward the women's prison. He seemed to know precisely where we were going. He left the path when we were almost at the prison, said "Mind the small nettles," and shortly afterward we came to a small clearing. Evidently someone had been there before us. The grass was trampled down around a crooked birch tree. All around us were bluebells, daisies, buttercups, and big white bunches of wild cow parsley.

We sat down, our backs against the tree. The dew was still on the grass so we spread out our jackets. Einar took an apple from the plastic bag he'd been carrying and gave it to me.

"I met this apple tree on my way through the village before I came to get you," he explained.

It must have been a great apple tree. The apple he gave me was transparently green and tasted incredibly good.

"You'll have to show me that tree some time," I said.

Einar promised to do that, then leaned back, slowly eating his apple.

We ate in silence, then each had another apple. I could feel the sun on my neck and could hear the bumblebees getting more lively. I threw the apple cores into the bluebells, then nearly fell asleep against the tree. I thought maybe we should start sleeping out here in the field.

Einar was busy pulling blades of grass. I gathered he hadn't dragged me out of bed this early just to eat apples or to sleep under a tree, so I waited patiently for him to tell me whatever it was he'd decided he wanted to tell. But it took time. And another apple. There were lots of them in the bag.

"I want to tell you about Vera," he said at last.

I only nodded, afraid to say anything that might upset him before he started.

"Vera lived with the Stenstad family for more than two years. And so did I. They were her eighth set of foster parents. I think her record for staying in one place was six months before she came there. She always ran away, or behaved so badly that no one could stand having her around. She really had the knack of getting away without anyone noticing, and she had friends who helped her. But she was always found and sent back. She must have been on the run when we met her that day downtown. She always talked about trying to stay hidden until she was so old they'd stop chasing her and leave her alone.

"There were three foster children at the Stenstads': a baby, Vera, and me. They had children of their own, too, who had grown up and had moved out. They were my first foster parents, and I didn't like it there. I didn't like the people who came to tell me why I had to stay there either, and I never did understand *why* I had to be there. I kept telling them all the time that I didn't want to be there, but nobody listened. Nobody cared. Except Vera."

Einar stopped, as if to catch his breath after a long run.

When he'd started his story, I had expected — no, I don't really know what I expected, but this wasn't at all what I'd thought I'd hear. It dawned on me in a very scary way that Einar hadn't woken me up to tell me about Vera. Not at all. Einar wanted to tell me what he'd never told another living soul — the secret hidden deep down inside him, the secret now burning on his tongue.

I hardly dared breathe or look at him as he sat there beside me, preparing himself to tell his story. The story of Einar Andersen.

F O U R T E E N

"MUM AND DAD were driving home after a movie in Oslo one Saturday night, around eleven. I was with Grandma and Granddad — they had a small farm then just outside Askim. It was a drunk driver, a head-on collision. The girl with him died the day after. He survived. Mum and Dad died on the spot.

"There was no telephone on the farm out there in the woods, and it takes half an hour just to go down to the main road. When the police finally arrived it was the middle of the night. The dog sensed them way before we could see them, so we were awake and standing by the window when they approached. There were two of them, and their flashlights made me think of a cross-eyed cat. At Christmas it will be five years.

"I stayed on the farm and never went home again. Grandma and Granddad went and got most of our things, then the flat in Askim was sold. It was best that way. I felt I could never go back. Some weeks later I started at a new school. It was a long way off, but I didn't mind. Living in the woods was good. Sometimes it felt as if we were sleepwalking, all three of us. But when evening came we were always together.

"We talked about Mum and Dad. They told me everything they remembered from when Mum and Dad were growing up. Mum's parents lived on a farm quite far away, but they didn't mind distances then, so Mum and Dad were always together. That's why my grandparents knew Mum as well as they knew Dad."

Einar stopped talking. The silence lasted several minutes.

"One day the child welfare authorities came and said I had to leave. They'd found me a foster family, they said. Why did I have to leave? I went to school every day. I hadn't done anything wrong. Grandma and Granddad hadn't done anything wrong.

80

"The authorities said Grandma and Granddad were too old to take care of me, that they
lived too far out of the way. It was bad for me to
live so isolated from other children. Granddad
said that his son, meaning my dad, had grown
up on the farm, and that people got used to
distances. A bit of a walk to the nearest neighbor had never harmed anyone. The authorities
locked their faces and went away, but the next
week they were back again."

Einar smiled an ugly little smile and went on.

"After that I met Mr. and Mrs. Stenstad. I
kicked and fought and spat, but the authorities
dragged me down to the main road, where a
police car was waiting. Did you know you can't
open the back doors of a police car from the
inside?

"Vera was there when I arrived. First thing I
did was run away. Home. But it didn't take
long before the police came and got me. Next
day I ran away again. Vera helped me then,
and ever since. This time it took me longer to
get a ride, so the police were already there
when I arrived. And the next time too, and the
next time, and the next . . .

"The authorities said that if I didn't stop running away they'd have to send me to a foster
home in another part of the country. Until I set-

tled down, Grandma and Granddad wouldn't be allowed to visit me. But Vera and I understood that if I did settle down everything would be lost. Because I desperately wanted to live with Grandma and Granddad. I didn't want them to *visit* me. I wanted to *live* with them.

"But I stopped running away. Couldn't take the risk. Vera hit on something that proved to be just as good: I stopped going to school. I went out every morning and hid until school was over. Some days they'd watch me, so I had to stay for the first or second lesson, but then I nearly always managed to get away. They couldn't very well tie me to my desk, could they, even though I'm sure they'd have done so gladly.

"They tried everything: locking me up in the house, no dinner, no pocket money, and so on and so forth. But nothing worked. Vera helped me. She'd used the method herself a couple of times, and was sure it would work again as long as we didn't give in. She promised she'd stay with the Stenstad family until I could go home. That meant she stopped running away. Well, almost. That is, only just playing truant a little from time to time, nothing much. I'd found some safe places in the woods, where I used to go during the day, and sometimes Vera would come too.

"There were always quarrels with the headmaster, with the family I lived with, and with the authorities, because I wouldn't go to school. I told them that the minute they let me go home I'd go to school every day, even Sundays if they wanted me to. But not until then. Never.

"I was constantly afraid they'd move me to another place, to another part of the country, or away from Vera, so I waited a full year before I dared go home again for a short secret visit no one knew about. Except Vera. It all went well because by now everybody was used to my running off every day. And they'd stopped looking in vain for me at my grandparents' months before.

"Remember you told me about Hewad yesterday? You said you'd thought about what it'd be like if you couldn't go home? I know a lot about that. Oh yes, I know about that! Do I ever!"

He didn't expect a comment, and I didn't give one.

He went on. "I didn't go back again. That was the only time I dared to go see my grandparents, but I was glad I did. They told me they'd hired a lawyer to help get me home again. We might have to move to get our way, but we wouldn't have to sell the farm. We could use the insurance money Mum and Dad left. And then we could go back to the farm during school holidays. They'd been told that I didn't go to school, and I explained why, and told them about Vera.

"They worked their end, and I worked mine, and after two years we made it. Grandma and Granddad bought the flat here at Veitvet, so we wouldn't live so far out in the country, and the authorities were fed up with my always refusing to go to school. I had to start in a lower grade when I came here, but I didn't care. It wasn't a high price to pay to have a real home again. Vera kept her promise and stayed with the Stenstad family until I was back with my grandparents. Then she vanished. I hadn't seen her until we met her downtown that morning."

Here Einar ended his story, and I thought I understood everything: why he always left things at my place, why he never complained about his grandparents being so old-fashioned and strict, and why he was so afraid of Hewad. Einar was afraid everything would be taken away from him again.

"We'll always be friends," I said.

"Will we?"

"Yes. And Hewad can't change that. Nobody can, for that matter. I think the three of us could have a lot of fun together."

"You think so?"

"Yes, I do. And it wouldn't make the two of us any less friends if we do. We can be brothers!" My words made me smile because I really wanted him to be my brother.

Einar smiled a little too. "Okay, let's be friends, then — and brothers. If it's possible."

"It is."

Then we got up and went back the same way we'd come, through the early summer morning. Einar in front, still carrying his plastic bag. We hadn't eaten all the apples.

We parted at the crossing above the subway. It would still be some time before Sunday really started and people got up, so we went to our different homes to wait.

"See you," I said.

"Yeah, later," Einar said.

"Two short and a long one," I said. And so we did.

F I F T E E N

DAD HAD TUESDAY off as well as the two following days. Every time Dad has days off in
the middle of a week — and it doesn't happen
often — Mum has one of her fits. We're getting
used to them now. It wasn't so easy in the beginning.

It starts off with Mum going down to the cellar to find her big blue-gray pottery jar. Then
she asks to be driven downtown to buy clay.
Dad always obliges without a word.

They carry the heavy jar between them up
the stairs, and once inside the door again Mum
moves into the kitchen. We have quite a large
kitchen, but when Mum's working there we

can hardly get to the fridge. We grab a slice of bread in a hurry, and dinner is something out of a tin or a bag. We have to eat in the living room because Mum has stacked all the kitchen chairs — except for the one she's using — and has laid an old door on top of the kitchen table. She hardly eats anything and lives solely on bread and tea as long as the fit lasts.

It's no use asking her what she's making. And if we try to peek, she snarls like a ferocious tiger, at least until she's really into it. Then she hardly notices us. We become invisible to her. She wouldn't notice if we vanished from the surface of Gaia. She wouldn't notice if I were to bring my whole class into my room and start a discotheque. She wouldn't hear a thing. In short, she's in another world as long as the fit lasts. But we've adjusted because we know it will pass. Her best pieces are on top of the bookcase in the living room. The best, or perhaps I should say the strangest. Because Mum's not one for making cups or dishes. No, she makes peculiar figures of clay that start you wondering.

The latest fit had been an especially rough one. She snarled like an angry dog whenever we touched the kitchen door, and she didn't speak to us for two days. Dad declared he was sick and tired of lukewarm spaghetti out of tins, and of camping in the living room. He invited me and Kara out to dinner and to the movies afterward. He'd be going back to work the next day, and we were all worried that Mum wouldn't be finished in time. Keeping our distance was definitely the wisest thing to do.

Dad and Kara were waiting for me by the subway when Einar, Hewad, and I were coming up Veitvetveien after school the next afternoon. After the incident at Tøyen the previous Saturday, Hewad seemed to have drawn closer to us, and he even seemed to be enjoying himself.

Einar went along with things, but it was hard to tell what he was really feeling. He hadn't referred to our morning trip to the Bredtvet Fields, and neither had I. I was sure we'd never talk about it again, now that everything had been said.

We parted with our usual two short and a long one. Hewad hadn't quite got the knack of it yet, so he started hiccupping instead. Einar was to take my bookbag to his place while Dad and Kara and I were in town. Einar has great respect for Mum's fits, which he refers to as expressions of her artistic nature.

Einar and Hewad went on up the hill together. Hewad was walking backward, waving to me. I saw him stumble, and he would've fallen if Einar hadn't put out an arm to support him. That was the last I saw of them before we went into the subway.

"Monica loves Thomas" was written in gold on the green seat beside me and dated two months earlier. Maybe she still loves him. I wondered who Thomas loves.

Kara demanded to see the toy department of Steen & Strøm, and to preserve domestic peace Dad agreed immediately.

The moment we entered the department store, Kara said she had to go to the toilet. Dad looked around. The ladies' room was on the second floor. It said so on the sign by the escalator. When we finally found the toilets, behind the women's underwear department, Kara refused to go inside alone.

Dad looked at me. I shook my head. No way.

"You have to come with me!" Kara shouted at Dad, who was beginning to get red in the face as people turned to stare.

"Okay, just take it easy," Dad said at last. "We'll have to go down to the men's room, because I can't go into the ladies'."

"Why can't you come in here with me?" Kara asked. "Mum always does."

Holy smoke! There were times I . . .

"Because," Dad answered.

"How come I can go with you to the men's room?" she persisted after a moment's consideration.

"Because," Dad answered.

"Okay, I see," Kara said. And then we went down the escalator again.

Luckily there was no one else in the men's room. Afterward Kara took a long time washing her hands. A very long time.

"I like water," she declared. "I'd like to take a bath."

"I thought you wanted to see the toys." By now I was getting fed up. And hungry.

"Mmmn, and I do. Now." But first she had to dry her hands. There were no paper towels, so she had to use the drier. I pressed the button. Warm air gushed out.

"It's boiling over!" Kara was howling with joy, laughing so hard she tripped over her shoelaces, which were untied, of course. And there she lay on the floor, shrieking with laughter. She didn't hurt herself, and was still giggling when we got her upright and tied her shoelaces for her.

"This is something I just have to tell Maren-Kristine Haug-Larsen: that it's boiling over in the men's room." Kara sounded like a contented little chicken.

Toys are dull, especially the ones Kara wanted to look at. I climbed up onto a rabbit, one of the ones where you put a krone in its ear and it pretends it's a horse and gallops as long as the money lasts. But it was out of order.

We were going to have Chinese food for dinner. I would kill for Chinese food. I had just made up my mind what I'd have for dessert when Dad and Kara finally came along. He'd bought Kara a little Playmo ghost figure.

"It glows in the dark," Kara explained.

At last, we were ready to leave.

"I want my dinner now," Dad said. "I just have to have a pee and then buy a newspaper."

I had to have one too. Kara stayed at the information desk under strict orders not to move an inch.

As Dad was about to pay for his newspaper, he met a man I'd never seen before and started talking to him. It took some time. In fact, it took ages. I'd read the headlines more than seventy-five times when I heard a woman's voice on the public address system saying, "There's a little girl of five here who's lost her dad and brother. Her name is — "

At this point, Kara must have grabbed the

microphone because her voice came over, loud and clear. "Where are you, Dad? You said you were only going to pee. What's taking you so long?"

Then there was static and the sounds of scuffling. It stopped abruptly and a total silence followed.

Dad said a hasty farewell to the man and raced, with me at his heels, back to the information desk. Kara was standing inside behind the counter talking urgently to a woman who was answering her with equal urgency. We couldn't hear what they were saying and that, I guess, was just as well.

"Come on, Kara. We're leaving." Dad whipped open the door and literally snatched Kara out of the booth. I felt so ashamed I could have died.

But we had Chinese food. I had baked bananas for dessert, and Kara was an angel the rest of the evening. We all laughed at the movie and Kara almost fell asleep on the subway on the way home.

As soon as we opened the door, we knew. Everything was calm, peaceful. The door to the kitchen was open, and inside things were back to normal. The floor was clean, the kitchen table and the chairs were in their usual

places, the large blue-gray jar was gone. A
newly picked bouquet of wild flowers was in
the white vase on the table. It was as if the last
three days had been only a dream. Except for
one thing: Beside the flowers there was something covered by a wet blue towel. Mum had
finished, thank heavens! I don't know what
would have happened otherwise.

She was lying on the sofa. I thought she was
asleep. She smiled at us when we came in, said
hi, and asked if we'd had a good time. We all
nodded yes without taking our eyes off her. We
waited — Dad, Kara, and I.

"You want to see?"

Once again we nodded, still afraid to say anything. But her way of asking told us she was
pleased with her work.

We followed her into the kitchen and
watched her lift away the blue towel. Beneath
it was the head of a young woman with short
straight hair. She was actually very beautiful
and had a strange, dreamy expression in her
eyes.

"She's lovely," Dad said.

Mum moved the head so we could see it in
profile. Behind the right ear the head was hol-
low, and inside was a little figure, the statue of a
woman sitting with her legs crossed and with

four arms reaching upward. The little figure reminded me of something, a picture I'd seen in a book somewhere, at school, I think.

Dad looked as if he'd seen a ghost. "But Lillian," he said. That must have been the only thing he could think of to say while he looked from the head of clay on the table over to Mum, again and again. "Oh, but Lillian."

I don't know what the figure reminded Dad of, but after I had gone to bed that night, I could hear their voices from the living room. They talked for hours. Their voices made me think of a waterfall a long way off. Then I went to sleep.

S I X T E E N

IN THE DAYS that followed, things went from good to better. Every day on the way to school I met Einar at the subway station, and Hewad was waiting for us at the corner of Beverveien.

Friday of the following week we were coming home from school, looking forward to a long weekend. We had decided we'd spend the weekend by the lake since Hewad hadn't been there yet. Hewad and I were talking. Einar walked silently beside us, but he wasn't cross or anything. The time for that was definitely gone. No, I'd say he seemed distant, as if he was doing something that required all his energy and attention. I smiled at him. He smiled back. Walking beside Einar, Hewad seemed even darker, but I guess I did too, come to think of it.

We decided to share a Coke and crossed the road below the bank.

They were standing outside the paint store. Some of them were sitting on the stairs. There were seven or eight men. Four plastic bags and some empty bottles were spread out around them. Two more bags of beer were standing beside the men sitting on the lower steps.

We three looked at each other, knowing the best thing to do was to get past them as fast as we could. They were already quite noisy, and I thought maybe they wouldn't pay any attention to us. But one of them grabbed hold of Hewad.

"Go back to where you came from! We don't want Pakis here."

I stopped dead. So did Einar.

"Let me go! I haven't done anything!" Hewad cried, struggling to get free. "And I'm not Pakistani. I'm from Afghanistan, and I couldn't go home even if I wanted to. My country is at war and we're fighting . . . "

Hewad had turned very pale, and I felt awful. I took hold of one of Hewad's arms and pulled to help him get away, shouting in anger and fear. "Stop it! Let him go! Don't touch my pal, you bastard!" My heart was beating so hard I thought it was going to explode, and all the time I was wondering if anything like this had happened to Hewad before.

The man held Hewad by the T-shirt. He was big and strong and very red in the face, and he wouldn't let go. Then he hit my arm so hard I had to let go of Hewad's arm, and he shoved me so that I fell on the stairs. I saw him jerk Hewad even closer to him as he shouted, "So, you wanna fight, you bloody Paki!" Then he hit Hewad on the cheek with such force that Hewad spun around and would have fallen if the man hadn't kept hold of him. "You came here to fight, did you?" The man hit Hewad a second time, this time so violently Hewad fell to the ground and lay motionless.

I rushed forward. What if Hewad was dead? What if the man had killed him?

"Are you okay?" I asked, and could have cried with relief when Hewad opened his eyes, looked at me, and said, "I'm not too bad." He touched his cheek and moaned. I'll never forget the way it sounded when the man's fist hit Hewad's face.

A crowd was gathering. It seemed to be growing all the time. A sharp voice said loudly that someone ought to call the police, but no one moved. They were all just standing there. Why didn't anyone help us?

"It's a shame nobody's doing anything. Why don't some of you help these kids?" a fat woman said. But the well-dressed man she'd spoken to shook his head and said he never interfered in a fight. And besides, it was none of his business.

"Oh, please, help us!" I cried, but the well-dressed man went on his way. He didn't care about us. No one did. The man with the red face gave me an evil smile once the well-dressed man was out of sight. Then I knew that if he had killed Hewad he wouldn't have cared. He'd only have grinned his ugly smile, and nobody else would have cared either.

I helped Hewad to his feet. He looked dizzy and scared, and I held on to him so he wouldn't fall. I was trembling. Why were all the grownups just standing there, watching? Why didn't anyone *do* anything?

That's when Einar went into action. Like a roaring animal, he sprang at the man with the ugly smile. Einar hit him once, then again. He was so fast there was no stopping him. The man was a giant, but there was Einar trying to knock him down! Einar. Did I ever really doubt Einar? Oh, no. Einar would always stand up for his friends.

Then Einar was lifted off the ground by a powerful arm.

"So, you're in his war too, you Paki lover," the man yelled.

Einar looked very small, but answered bravely that yes, he was. Then the man took deliberate aim and punched Einar in the nose. He fell to the ground with blood streaming down his pale face.

"Einar!"

We spoke at the same time, Hewad and I, and together we bent down to help him up. Einar tried to mop up the blood running from his nose, but he only made it worse, and afterward he looked really awful. But he gave us a faint smile when he was back on his feet again.

The man showed no intention of ending the fight yet. I looked around. The gang with the plastic bags was still sitting on the lower steps, like a pile of dead flies. And the crowd of spectators had grown even bigger.

"Why don't you help us?" I cried out to them just as the man tried to kick Hewad but missed.

"Little black rat! You can't even speak proper Norwegian!" he shouted, but not as

99

loud as before. Einar's blows had obviously knocked some of the air out of him.

The words startled me. What the man said was like an echo of something I'd heard before, something very important, something I *had* to remember.

That's when Dad came. Shouting, he pushed his way through the crowd, shoving so hard that people jumped out of the way before they knew what hit them. Behind Dad came Hewad's father. Then I knew what the important thing was that I had to remember. And I had to make Dad understand. I had to.

Dad rushed up and grabbed all three of us, me and Hewad and Einar, and held us close. Then Hewad's father was there, holding us too.

"It's all over now," Dad murmured into my hair, and it felt good. But it wasn't over yet. There was one more thing left to do.

"Dad, Dad," I said anxiously. "Isn't it true that Hewad speaks proper Norwegian, just like you do?"

Dad looked at me inquiringly for a moment that lasted a whole eternity, then he smiled and in his country dialect said, "Hewad's a nice guy and he speaks just the way he should. There's nothing wrong with him, not in the least. You get away from here!" he addressed the man with the red face. "And stop pestering people who've done no harm to you or any of yours."

Dad! He understood!

While he was talking I could smell the flowers of the summer meadows at Kapp and I could see Mjøsa glittering across the road. My dad is the best dad in the whole wide world. I've always known that.

The man had stayed quiet for a while but now he was approaching again, trying out an angry fist against Dad, who met the blow like an experienced boxer and sent him right into the arms of Hewad's father, who pushed him head forward into the gang sitting on the lower steps. Then they'd had enough. The whole group withdrew from the battlefield on unsteady feet, with a clattering and rattling of beer bottles in plastic bags. By now the spectators were drifting off too, and the two fathers were standing there looking at each other. Finally, there were only the five of us left on the scene.

I haven't the slightest idea if Hewad's father had understood any of what Dad had said, but it was obvious he'd grasped the meaning behind the words, because he reached out his right hand and in perfect Afghan-Norwegian said, "You are my brother."

Dad held out his right hand too, and they

shook hands and patted each other's shoulders and smiled the biggest smiles I'd seen that day.

"This calls for a celebration," said Hewad's father. "You must come and have dinner with us tonight."

Dad accepted the invitation at once. He was beaming with delight. Whether it was because he had a new brother or because the battle had been won and the enemy driven away, I can't say.

"Einar has to come too," I said. "If it hadn't been for him, we'd all be dead now."

"You're a very brave young man," said Hewad's father, and we all nodded in agreement. "It will be a great honor if you would dine with us tonight."

Einar smiled from behind all the blood smeared over his face, assuring us all that yes, he would like to come.

"Let's say seven o'clock, then. And you must bring your family," Hewad's father said to Dad.

"That'll be fine," Dad answered. "We'd like that very much. By the way," he said, "did you understand any of what I said back there?"

"Not a single word," Hewad's father answered. "Tell me, can't you speak proper Norwegian, or what?"

They both roared with laughter. When they

finally stopped and caught their breath, Hewad and his father went down the hill. Dad, Einar, and I went up.

"I forgot my blue sweatshirt at your place yesterday," Einar said to me. "I'll come with you now and get it."

"What!" I stopped so suddenly I nearly fell on my face. "But you can come and get it tomorrow."

"I know that," Einar smiled, his head bent. "And I'll come tomorrow, too."

Holy smoke!

Hewad still can't do two short and a long one — but he keeps trying.